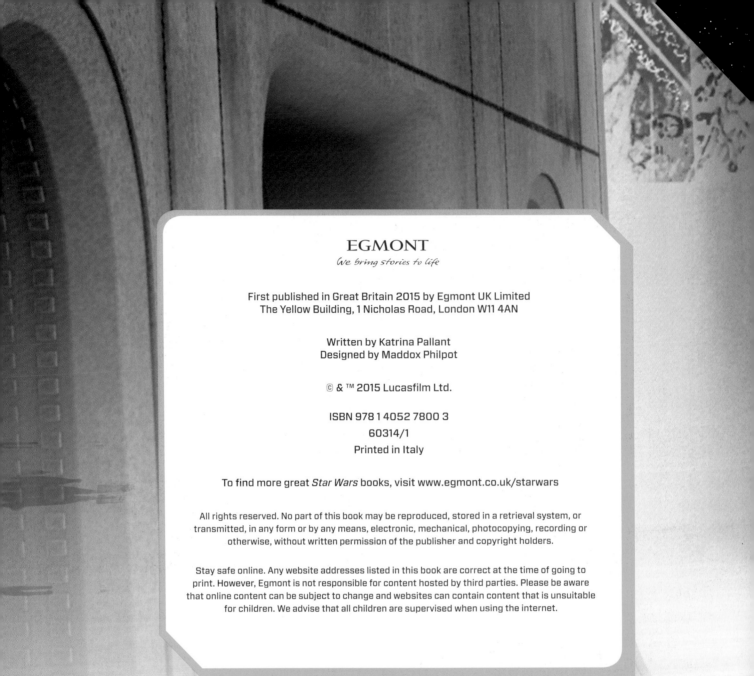

EGMONT

We bring stories to life

First published in Great Britain 2015 by Egmont UK Limited
The Yellow Building, 1 Nicholas Road, London W11 4AN

Written by Katrina Pallant
Designed by Maddox Philpot

© & ™ 2015 Lucasfilm Ltd.

ISBN 978 1 4052 7800 3

60314/1

Printed in Italy

To find more great *Star Wars* books, visit www.egmont.co.uk/starwars

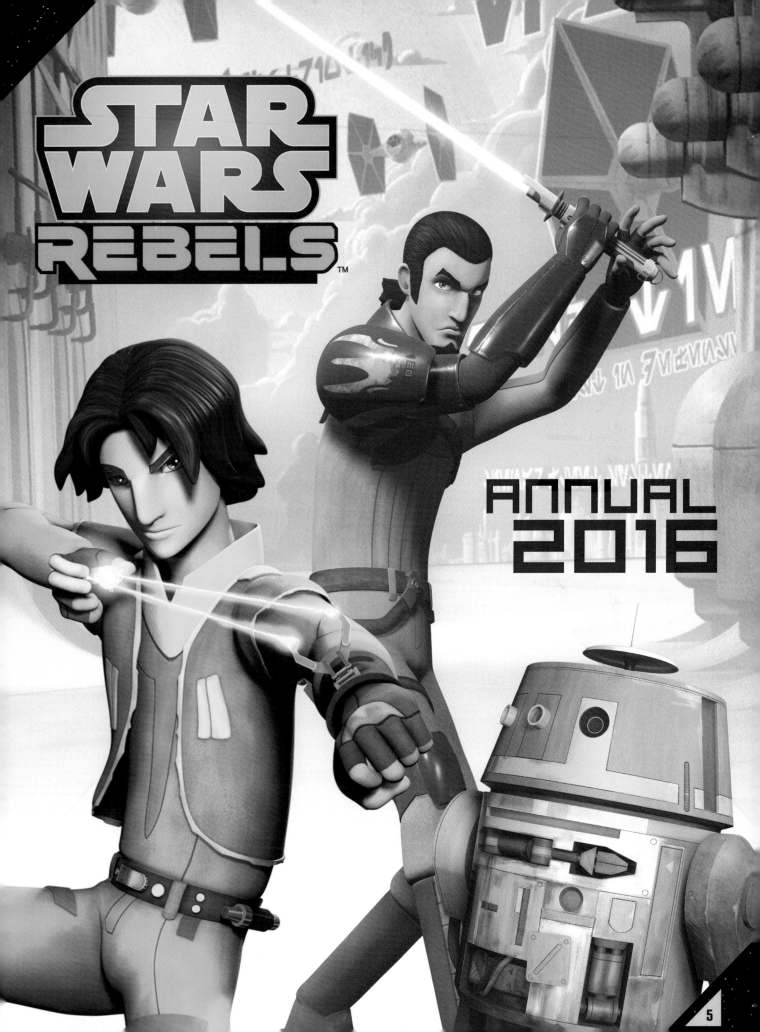

CONTENTS

WELCOME TO THE REBELLION

During a dark a time for the galaxy, when the Empire has complete control, a small group of rebels bring hope to the people of Lothal.

Disrupting Imperial missions with pranks, hijacking and general mischief, the crew of the *Ghost* fight the government and aim to bring freedom to the residents of this outer-rim planet.

JOIN THIS REBELLIOUS GROUP BY FILLING IN YOUR STATS BELOW.

Name:

Age:

Species:

Home planet:

Special weapon:

Vehicle of choice:

Best friend:

Name of droid:

Worst enemy:

LOTHAL LONER

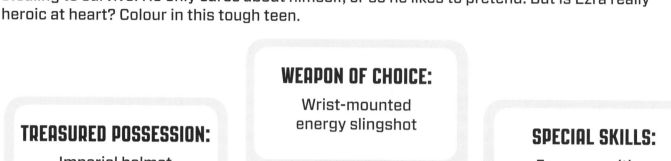

Meet Ezra Bridger. Ezra lost his family to the Empire, and lives alone on the streets of Lothal, stealing to survive. He only cares about himself, or so he likes to pretend. But is Ezra really heroic at heart? Colour in this tough teen.

WEAPON OF CHOICE:
Wrist-mounted energy slingshot

TREASURED POSSESSION:
Imperial helmet collection

SPECIAL SKILLS:
Force-sensitive, master of deception

Ezra lives in an abandoned communications tower, perfect for secrets and protection from the Empire. Draw your own sky-high hiding place here.

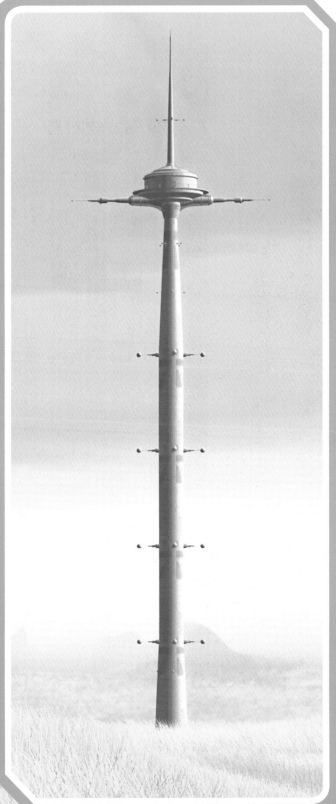

Kanan Jarrus

is the leader of the *Ghost* crew. He was training to be a Jedi in the old Republic, but now his only purpose is to bring down the Empire. He is loyal and protective of his team.

Weapon of choice:
Blue lightsaber, but also skilled with a pistol
Special skills:
Expert wielder of a lightsaber, telekinesis

Hera Syndulla

is a Twi'lek from Ryloth, who pilots the *Ghost*. She is an excellent schemer, and uses it to make Imperials' lives very difficult. She is reliable and holds the *Ghost* crew together.

Weapon of choice:
Hera uses the *Ghost* to outmanoeuvre TIE fighters and has an excellent aim with the *Ghost*'s guns
Special skills:
Ace pilot, skilled shooter

Zeb Orrelios

is the muscle of the group. He loves nothing more than punching stormtroopers and causing chaos to the Empire's regime. He may seem a bit difficult, but he'd do anything for his family.

Weapon of choice:
Bo-rifle – the traditional weapon of the Lasat Honour Guard, protectors of the planet Lasan.
Special skills:
Hand-to-hand combat, heightened strength

The *Ghost*

is a light freighter that serves as a home base for the rebels. It has a variable transponder signature that allows it to assume false identities when picked up on enemy scanners. This means it can disappear and reappear in the same place and the Imperials won't recognise it!

COLOUR IN THE *REBELS* FAMILY

Chopper

is the *Ghost* crew's grumpy, but helpful, droid. He fixes the ship and provides technical support for missions.

Special skills:
Astrogation, starship repair

Sabine Wren

is a Mandalorian girl with tons of creative energy. She specialises in explosives that leave a signature mark, so all the Imperials will know she has been there.

Weapon of choice:
Explosives, but also handy with a pistol in a pinch
Special skills:
Stealth – can leave her vibrant graffiti without getting caught

THE LOYAL IMPERIALS

Agent Kallus

is a member of the Imperial Security Bureau, and his job is to monitor the loyalty of the citizens of Lothal. He is a fierce enforcer of the Empire's laws, and a smart and dangerous foe of the rebels.

Weapon of choice: Kallus carries a traditional Lasat weapon, which he took when he helped destroy Lasan. This makes him Zeb's mortal enemy.
Special skills: Hand-to-hand combat, skilled pilot

The Inquisitor

is a Pau'an with a menacing face. He is a trained interrogator and will not stop until he has tracked down all remaining Jedi. He is the rebels' trickiest opponent yet.

Weapon of choice: Unique double-ended lightsaber that he can spin and throw in combat
Special skills: Force-sensitive, advanced intelligence

TIE fighters

are easily recognisable by the roar of their engines. The pilots of these intimidating vessels are not to be messed with.

COLOUR IN THESE IMPERIAL TROOPS

Stormtroopers

on Lothal were recruited by the Empire following the Clone Wars. They are usually poorly equipped, and often defeated by the rebels.

Special equipment:
Imposing white armour, comlink in helmet, blaster pistol, thermal detonator

THE HEIST

1. In the crowded marketplace, in the Capital City of Lothal, two Imperial officers named Commandant Aresko and Taskmaster Grint are harassing a fruit seller. "All trade must be registered with the Empire," says Aresko.

"I remember what it was like before you Imperials ruined Lothal," the fruit seller replies. Aresko speaks into his comlink. "I'm bringing in a citizen under a charge of treason."

Ezra, a young street urchin, overhears this conversation and distracts Aresko long enough to steal his comlink. "All Officers to the main square! This is a **CODE RED EMERGENCY**," Ezra cries into the radio. The Imperials abandon the fruit seller, leaving him very relieved.

He thanks Ezra, but is shocked when the kid steals his fruit. "Hey, a kid's gotta eat," Ezra says as he disappears over the rooftops.

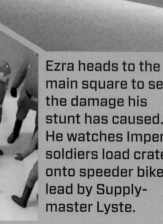

Ezra heads to the main square to see the damage his stunt has caused. He watches Imperial soldiers load crates onto speeder bikes, lead by Supply-master Lyste.

Just then, Ezra sees a mysterious man in the alley below. He watches the man meet up with a large Lasat and a girl in a Mandalorian helmet.

The girl then walks past the speeder bikes throwing something towards them. As she walks away the bike **EXPLODES!**

BOOOOOOM!

"GET THOSE CRATES OUT OF HERE! KEEP THEM SECURE, AT ALL COSTS!" Lyste shouts. The troopers take off on the speeder bikes, but their way is blocked by the rebel leader, Kanan. He jumps from his vehicle and kicks one of the troopers off his bike. The Lasat, Zeb, emerges from the alleyway and joins the fight.

Meanwhile, Ezra has seen the perfect opportunity to get his hands on one of the crates and jumps down onto one of the speeder bikes. "Thanks for doing the heavy lifting!" he calls to the rebel group before taking off. **"AFTER THAT KID!"** Kanan cries.

10.

The Mandalorian girl, Sabine, jumps down from a rooftop onto Ezra's bike. "Pretty gutsy move, kid! If the big guy catches you, he'll end you! Good luck!" She detaches one of the crates.

11.

Kanan and Zeb, pursued by troopers, trail after Ezra. They blast the troopers as Ezra dodges obstacles and people. "**WHO IS THIS KID?**" the rebel leader asks, amazed by his reflexes.

12.

The chase continues down the freeway. Ezra's bike is hit by Imperial walker fire and he loses control. As he swings into oncoming traffic, the rebels fight off the stormtroopers.

13.

Kanan detaches the crate from his own bike, and stops Ezra from escaping. "Who are you?" Ezra asks. "I'm the guy who was stealing that crate. I have plans for it, so today's not your day," Kanan replies.

"Day's not over." Ezra smiles smugly as a TIE fighter bears down behind them. Kanan jumps from his bike to avoid the TIE's fire, and Ezra speeds away.

The TIE fighter pursues Ezra. "Whatever's in these crates better be worth it!"
Ezra is hit and he flies off his bike, landing safely on the grass.

The TIE approaches when suddenly it is **BLASTED** out of the sky!

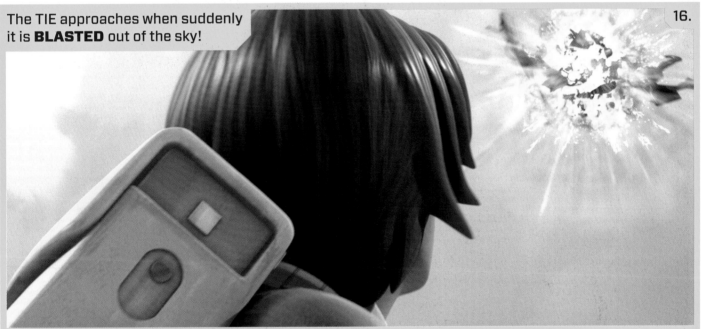

A large freighter flies in, hovers over Ezra and opens its cargo doors to reveal Kanan. "**YOU WANT A RIDE?**" he shouts from the *Ghost*.

As further TIEs approach, Ezra grabs the crate and runs towards the *Ghost*. "Leave the crate, you'll never make it!" Kanan cries. He watches in awe as Ezra leaps through the air with the crate in his hand and lands on the edge of the ship. Ezra pulls himself up and goes inside with Kanan.

CONTINUES ON PAGE 26 ⫸⫸⫸⫸⫸⫸⫸⫸

MARKETPLACE MINDBENDERS

When Ezra sees Imperial officers bullying a local street vendor, he tricks the troopers to help.
The vendor is very grateful. Help this hero with the below brainteasers.

1. CAN YOU GET FROM TRICK TO THANK BY CHANGING ONLY ONE LETTER AT A TIME?

TRICK

THANK

2. HOW MANY WORDS CAN YOU MAKE FROM THE PHRASE 'LOTHAL MARKETPLACE'? THERE ARE SOME BELOW TO GET YOU STARTED.

THAT

PARK

TALL

KEEP

3. WHO DOES EZRA HELP? UNSCRAMBLE THE WORDS TO FIND OUT.

RSEETT RVNEOD

SPEED SKETCH

The rebels and Imperials use lightweight speeder bikes to navigate the streets of Lothal. Draw your own bike here with either rebel or Imperial logos.

CRATE CONUNDRUM

It is hard to remain unseen when stealing crates from Imperial officers, but the rebels are determined to do it! Can you find the following hidden characters in the scene?

ZEB

CHOPPER

KANAN

EZRA

HERA

SABINE

WHO IS THAT KID?

Ezra is causing the rebels trouble by interrupting their mission and stealing the crates they wanted. Can you draw this picture of the mischief-maker in the right order in the grid?

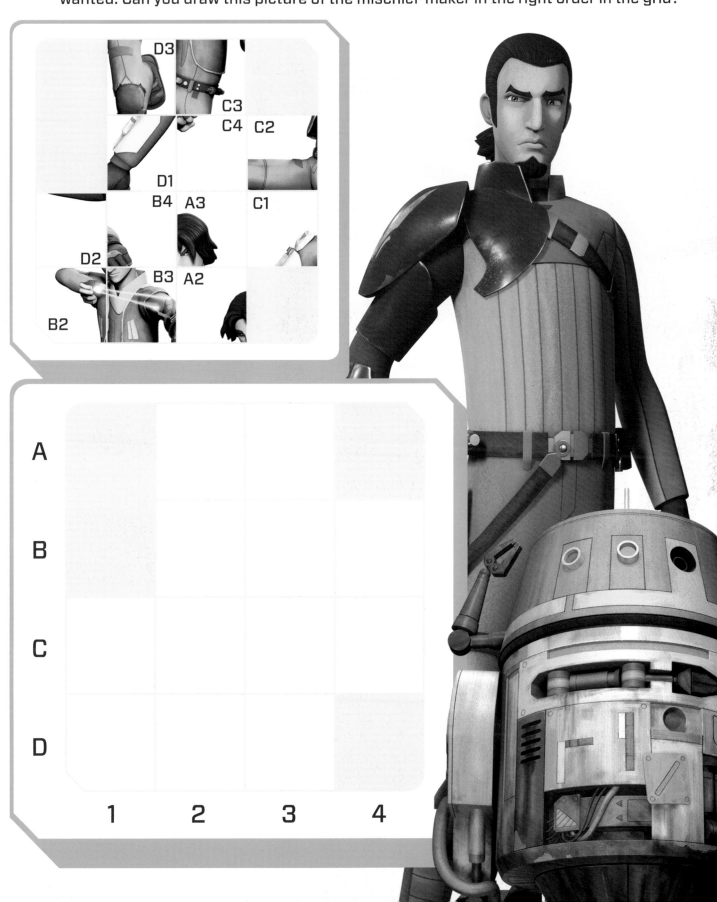

A

B

C

D

1   2   3   4

HOT PURSUIT

Ezra is being chased by the rebels and the troopers! Find five differences between these two pictures.

CARGO CAPER

Ezra wants to hijack a crate of Imperial cargo - but Kanan and the crew of the *Ghost* want it too! While the Imperial troops are focused on the rebels, Ezra can pass the Empire symbols safely. Help him find his way to the crate without running into Kanan's gang.

EMPIRE

REBELS

Ezra's made it to the crate, and now joins forces with the rebel crew. Guide him back to the *Ghost* - this time, you can pass the rebel symbols safely, but must avoid Imperial troops. Good luck!

THE NEWCOMER

CONTINUED FROM PAGE 17

1.

"**WHAT HAPPENED DOWN THERE?** We've got four TIE fighters closing in!" shouts Hera, the *Ghost*'s pilot, as Kanan joins her in the cockpit.

2.

Kanan tells Hera about Ezra, and shows her the cargo bay on the surveillance screen where Zeb and Sabine are supposed to be guarding the crates of Imperial blasters and the new arrival. Instead he sees an empty cargo bay.

3.

"Zeb, Sabine. Where's the kid?" he says into the intercom. Suddenly a TIE fighter screams into view, rocking the *Ghost* with a massive blast.

4.

"Woah!" Ezra cries, dropping out of the ventilation shaft he had escaped into. He lands in the gun turret, looking up to find himself in outer space for the first time in his life. He watches in awe until he sees the TIE fighters coming towards the ship. **"I'M ABOUT TO DIE!"**

5.

Kanan jumps into the gun-seat and starts firing at the Imperial opponents. Ezra watches stunned as Kanan blows up a TIE. The *Ghost* escapes into hyperspace, leaving the remaining TIE fighters in the dust.

6.

Back at the Main Square, Aresko is telling his superior, Agent Kallus about the heist.
"They knew our protocol and were waiting in position," Aresko says.
"It could signify the spark of rebellion," Agent Kallus warns them. "Next time they make a move, we'll be waiting for them."

7.

As the *Ghost* exits hyperspace Zeb drags Ezra into the cockpit.
"**TAKE ME BACK TO LOTHAL!**" demands Ezra.
"Just drop me and my blasters outside Capital City and –"
"They're not your blasters," Sabine chimes in.
"And we're not going back to Capital City," Kanan says. "The job's not done."

8.

The *Ghost* lands outside a small town of refugees.
"Lived on Lothal my whole life," Ezra says. "Never been here."
"The Imperials don't advertise it," Sabine explains. "They kicked these folks off their farms when the Empire wanted their land."

9.

The rebels deliver the blasters to a crime boss named Cikatro Vizago.
Vizago begins to count out credits to pay Kanan, but stops and offers them some intel on some Imperial prisoners instead.
"The Wookiees?" Hera asks excitedly.
Vizago smiles.

10.

The rebels then open the remaining crates revealing food for the refugees. **"WHO WANTS FREE GRUB?!"** Zeb calls. Ezra is stunned by this act of generosity, and backs away to sit by himself next to the *Ghost*.

11.

Ezra is drawn towards the ship, compelled by some unknown energy. He heads down the main corridor and, not realising that Chopper, the ship's droid, is watching, Ezra breaks into a locked bedroom.

12.

Ezra looks around the bedroom until he discovers a hidden panel on the bunk. He opens a drawer revealing a strange device. He pockets it, thinking it might be worth something. He reaches back into the draw and pulls out ... **A LIGHTSABER!** Kanan appears in the doorway. "Hand me the lightsaber. And get out."

13.

Kanan summons the group to the common room. Zeb orders Chopper, the droid, to keep watch on Ezra. "We have a new mission. Vizago acquired the flight plan for an Imperial Transport Ship full of Wookiee prisoners."

14.

Kanan pauses in the middle of describing his plan, reaching over to open a door to the supply area. Ezra tumbles down to the floor.
"Can we please get rid of him?" Zeb complains. "We don't have time to take him home. We need to move now." Hera agrees to keep an eye on Ezra during the mission.

15.

The *Ghost* approaches the Imperial Transport Ship. Speaking over the intercom, the Imperial Captain asks Hera what the *Ghost* is doing here. "We captured an additional Wookiee prisoner and have transfer orders to place him with you," she replies. "Permission to dock. Bay One."

16.

Kanan and Sabine escort Zeb in binders onto the ship, meeting some troopers at the airlock.
"**THAT THING'S NOT A WOOKIEE,**" one of the troopers says. Zeb quickly breaks free of his binders and punches both troopers with one swing.

17.

Back in the cockpit, the radio suddenly goes dead. "Spectre-1, come in," Hera calls. "Spectre-4? Spectre-5? Comm's down. No, not down. **JAMMED.**"
Ezra freezes. "Something's coming." "**THAT'S AN IMPERIAL STAR DESTROYER!**" Hera cries. The Star Destroyer approaches the transport and docks. Agent Kallus and a unit of stormtroopers prepare to board.

18.

"**THIS WHOLE THING WAS A SET-UP!**" Ezra shouts.
"You need to board the transport and warn them!" Hera cries.
"**NO, NO WAY!** Why would I risk my life for a bunch of strangers?"
"Because Kanan risked his for you."

CONTINUES ON PAGE 38

REBEL ORDER

Work out who comes next in the below sequences and draw the correct character in the box.

1.  ▶  ▶  ▶  ▶  ▶

2.  ▶ ▶  ▶  ▶  ▶

3.  ▶  ▶  ▶  ▶  ▶

4.  ▶  ▶  ▶  ▶  ▶

SPACE SQUABBLE

Hera and Kanan are always bickering. What does Kanan say when he returns to the *Ghost* with Ezra? Scribble out the letters indicated by the numbers to reveal the phrase.

	1	2	3	4	5	6	7	8	9
2, 4, 6, 8	A	B	L	R	I	E	T	S	T
1, 3, 4, 7	Q	L	R	L	E	L	M	E	S
2, 5, 8	S	R	A	T	P	T	I	N	T
1, 3, 5, 6	V	U	O	D	I	B	E	A	L
2, 5, 6, 8	I	F	T	T	W	O	L	G	E
3, 6, 7, 8	M	O	N	R	E	E	T	P	A
1, 3, 4, 6, 8, 9	S	L	J	D	T	X	I	Z	Y
2, 5, 7, 8, 9	T	A	U	D	R	E	V	D	S

ANSWER

____

____

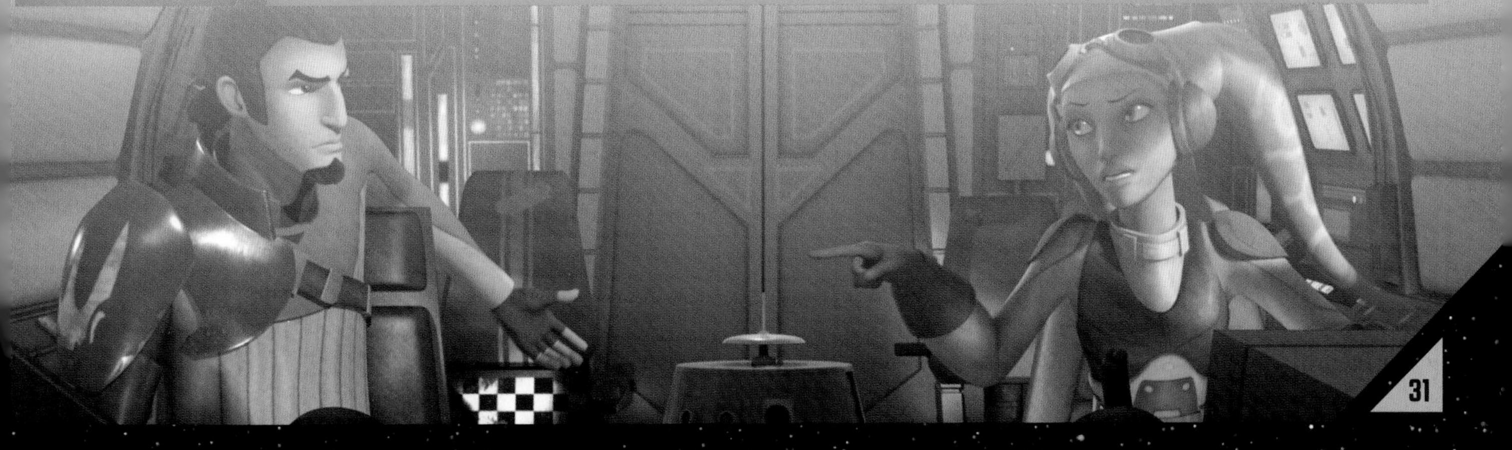

STORY TRIVIA PART ONE

Time to see what you remember about the story so far.

1. Where does Ezra live?

LOTHAL   **BESPIN**   **ALDERAAN**

(circle the right answer)

2. What colour is Hera?

3. What is the rebel leader called?

_____

4. What is the name of the black market dealer the rebels sell their weapons to?

ARESKO   **LYSTE**   **VIZAGO**

(circle the right answer)

5. The *Ghost* can scramble its signature. True or False?

TRUE ◯   **FALSE** ◯

6. The black market dealer gives the rebels Intel about which species?

TWI'LEKS   **WOOKIEES**   **LASATS**

(circle the right answer)

The rebels have a lot to say about the *Ghost*'s new passenger. Swap every letter with the one two before it in the alphabet to find out what the rebels think of Ezra.

A B C D E F G H I J K L M N O P Q R S T U V W X Y Z

TGEMNGUU

_____

ETGCVKXG

_____

IWVUA

_____

CPPQAKPI

_____

RUNAWAY REBEL

The rebels have lost Ezra in the vents of the *Ghost*. Which line will lead Zeb to the crafty kid?

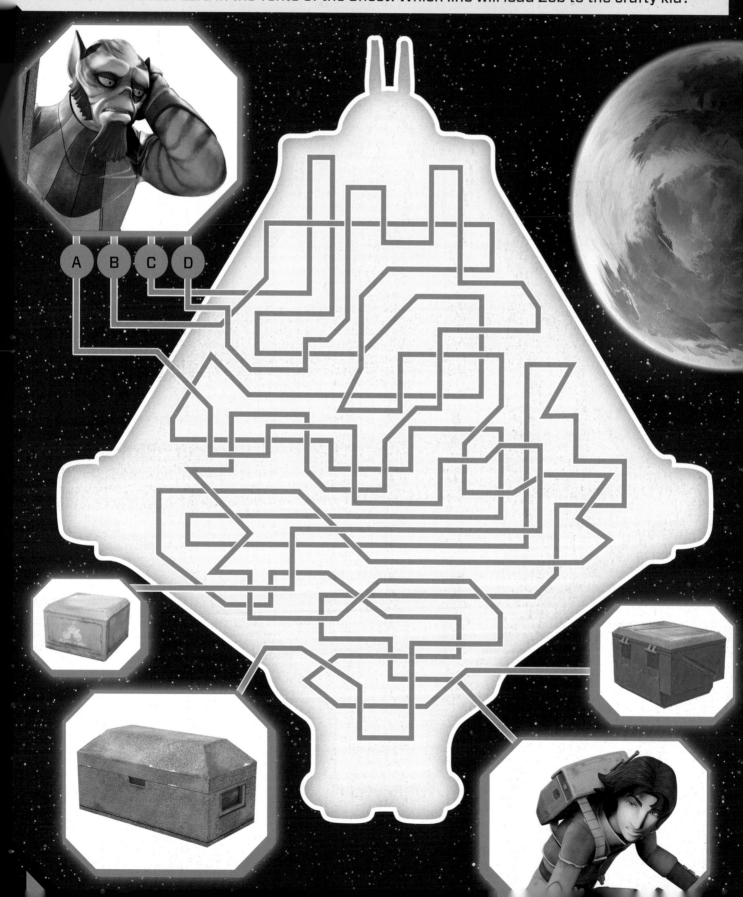

TWIN TROUBLEMAKERS

Zeb and Ezra bicker and fight when they first meet, but this feisty duo has a lot in common. Can you find the real Zeb and Ezra in these pictures?

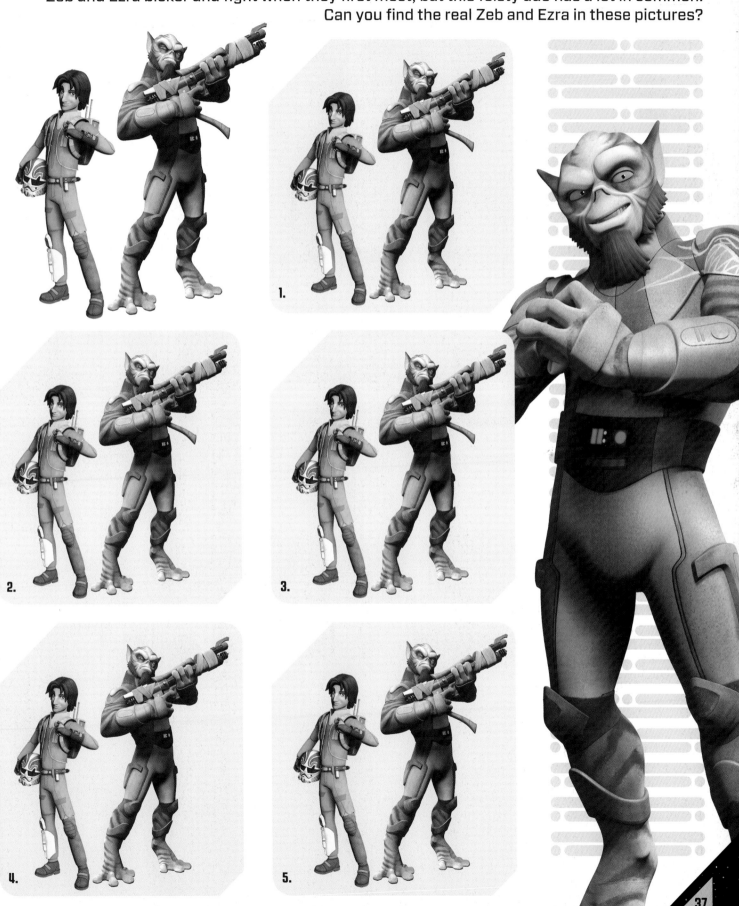

1.

2.

3.

4.

5.

THE TRAP

CONTINUED FROM PAGE 29

1.

The Star Destroyer approaches the Imperial transport where Kanan, Zeb and Sabine are currently trespassing. Hera pleads with the reluctant Ezra. "Our crew have no idea they walked into a trap. You need to go warn them, Ezra!"
"I CAN'T BELIEVE I'M DOING THIS!" Ezra cries as he stands up and exits the cockpit.

2.

Agent Kallus, along with a platoon of stormtroopers, enters the Imperial Transport with his blaster rifle at the ready.
"Welcome aboard, Agent Kallus," the captain says. "The rebels are headed for the brig – where quite the surprise awaits."

3.

Zeb and Kanan set detonators on the brig door so that they can free the Wookiees. Suddenly Ezra comes tearing in screaming, **"IT'S A TRAP! We gotta get out of here."**

4.

The door opens revealing the army of stormtroopers. **"RUN!"** Ezra yells. Kanan and Zeb take off down the corridor while Ezra holds off the troopers with his slingshot.

Elsewhere, in the gravity control station, Sabine and Chopper are at work. Sabine releases the controls and plunges the ship into low gravity settings. She and Chopper begin to plant explosives around the ship.

6.

Kanan, Zeb and Ezra leap forward in the low gravity. The unprepared troopers float around unable to take aim. Kanan fires at the troopers, and Kallus fires back.

7.

The rebels all land gracefully as the gravity kicks back in. Kanan, Zeb and Ezra run into the docking bay where the *Ghost*, Sabine and Chopper are waiting. "Where are the Wookiees?" Sabine asks. "**NO WOOKIEES!**" Kanan shouts.

8.

As the group board the ship, Zeb pushes Ezra out of the way so he can get in first. Ezra is yanked from behind by Kallus. The *Ghost* is attacked by dozens of troopers, and Zeb realises he has no choice but to leave Ezra behind. "Sorry kid. You did good." Zeb disappears behind the closing airlock doors.

9.

The *Ghost* detaches from the transport. **"CHOP, JAM THEIR TRACTOR BEAM!"** Hera shouts.

Over the radio the transport captain demands they surrender. "This is your first and last warning." "Blow it out your exhaust vent," Hera laughs. Sabine hits a button detonating her explosives. The *Ghost* is able to escape.

10.

The *Ghost* enters hyperspace and the rebels all sigh with relief.
"The whole thing was a set-up," Kanan says.
"You think Vizago was in on it?" Sabine asks.
"We're a source of income for him.
Even odds he didn't know," Hera replies.

11.

"The kid did all right," she continues, proud of Ezra's selflessness.
"He did okay," Kanan agrees.
"Where is he?" Everyone turns to Zeb.
"That I.S.B. Agent grabbed him," Zeb says, feeling guilty. "They'll go easy on him. He's just a kid … "

12.

Meanwhile, on the Star Destroyer, Agent Kallus is in Ezra's cell. "I am Agent Kallus of the Imperial Security Bureau. And you are?" "**JABBA THE HUTT,**" Ezra jokes. "Look, I just met those guys today. I don't know anything." "You're not here for what you know, 'Jabba'. You're here to be used as bait upon our return to Lothal."

13.

"**BAIT?**" Ezra laughs. "They're not gonna come for me! People don't do that." Kallus turns to his troopers. "Search him. Then secure him here." The troopers take Ezra's backpack containing his slingshot, his astromech arm and other tools.

14.

Ezra pulls the strange device that he took from Kanan's bedroom out of his pocket. "And of course, the only thing I manage to hold on to is this worthless piece … " He throws it across the cell in frustration. The device – which turns out to be a holocron, an old communication device – opens up like a flower and projects a hologram of Jedi Knight, **OBI-WAN KENOBI**.

15.

"I regret to report that both our Jedi Order and the Republic have fallen – with the dark shadow of the Empire rising to take their place." The hologram continues, "This message is a warning and a reminder for any surviving Jedi: **TRUST IN THE FORCE** … "

CONTINUES ON PAGE 50

GHOST GRID

Fill the gaps with the right rebel numbers making sure there is only one of each number in every row, column and box.

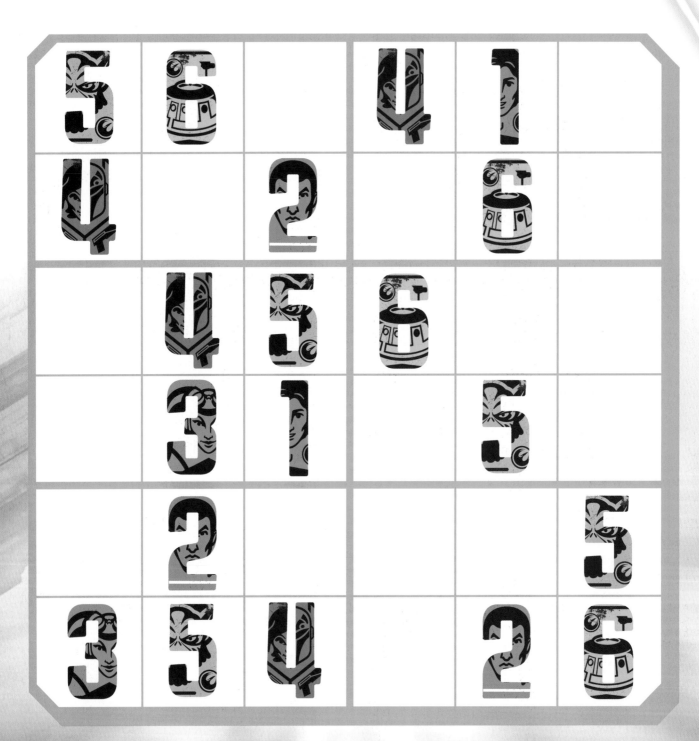

LIGHTSABER SUMS

As a Jedi, Kanan is in possession of a very unique weapon.
Do the sums and follow the right answers to find out which weapon is his.

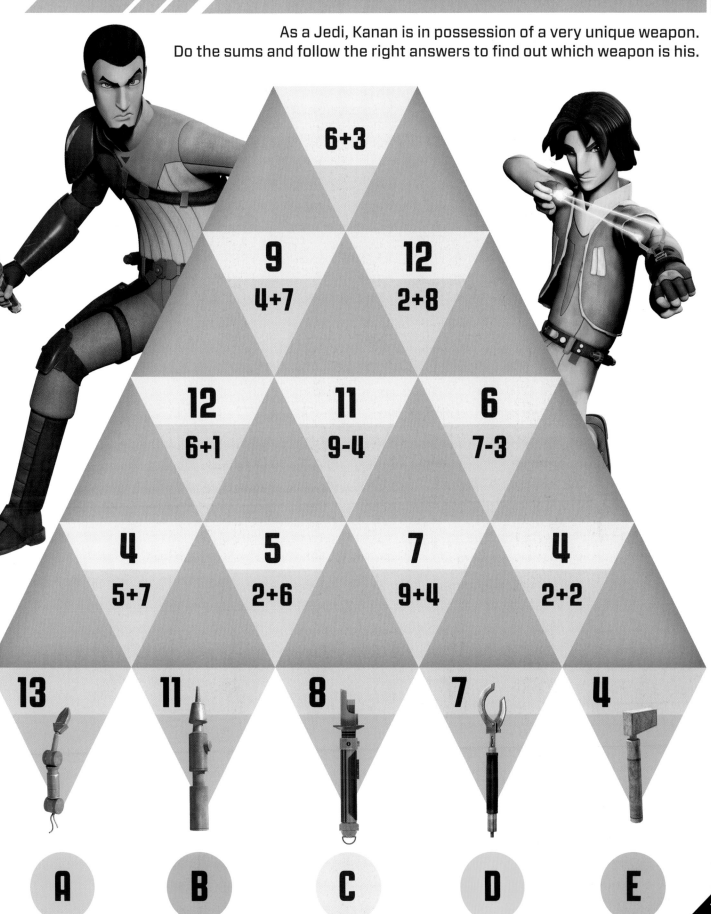

6+3

9
4+7

12
2+8

12
6+1

11
9-4

6
7-3

4
5+7

5
2+6

7
9+4

4
2+2

13

11

8

7

4

A **B** **C** **D** **E**

WHAT'S YOUR WEAPON?

Answer the questions to discover your Empire-fighting rebel weapon.

WHAT'S YOUR FAVOURITE COLOUR?

- A) Blue
- B) Orange
- C) Green
- D) Purple

WHO'S YOUR FAVOURITE REBEL?

- A) Kanan
- B) Ezra
- C) Zeb
- D) Sabine

WHERE DO YOU WANT TO LIVE?

- A) Coruscant
- B) Lothal
- C) Lasan
- D) Mandalore

WHAT REBEL JOB DO YOU WANT?

- A) Leader
- B) Con artist
- C) Muscle
- D) Technical support

WHO IS YOUR WORST ENEMY?

- A) Inquisitor
- B) Commandant Aresko
- C) Agent Kallus
- D) Stormtroopers

IF YOU GOT -

Mostly As: The perfect weapon for you is a lightsaber. This is a very special device for disciplined and focussed people.

Mostly Cs: The perfect weapon for you is a bo-rifle. You are always ready to jump into the fight.

Mostly Bs: The perfect weapon for you is a slingshot. You are sneaky and highly skilled.

Mostly Ds: The perfect weapon for you is explosives. You like to be creative and enjoy fireworks.

DRAW YOUR OWN WEAPON

Now you know what your ideal weapon is, draw it here! Or make up one of your own.

USE THE FORCE

Ezra discovers a weapon from a more civilized age. Use the Force to put this picture back together, writing the letter of each puzzle piece in the correct space.

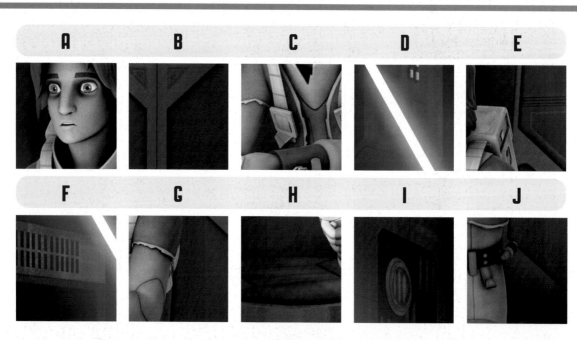

FOLLOW THE FORCE

Ezra feels the Force pulling him towards a special weapon, but which room is it in? Follow the directions and navigate around the map to see where he ends up.

Head out of the cockpit and turn left. Take a right past the Hangar then another right past Room A. Turn left and head towards the turret then take a right past the kitchen. Turn left and head to the very end of the corridor and enter the room on your left. **Where are you?**

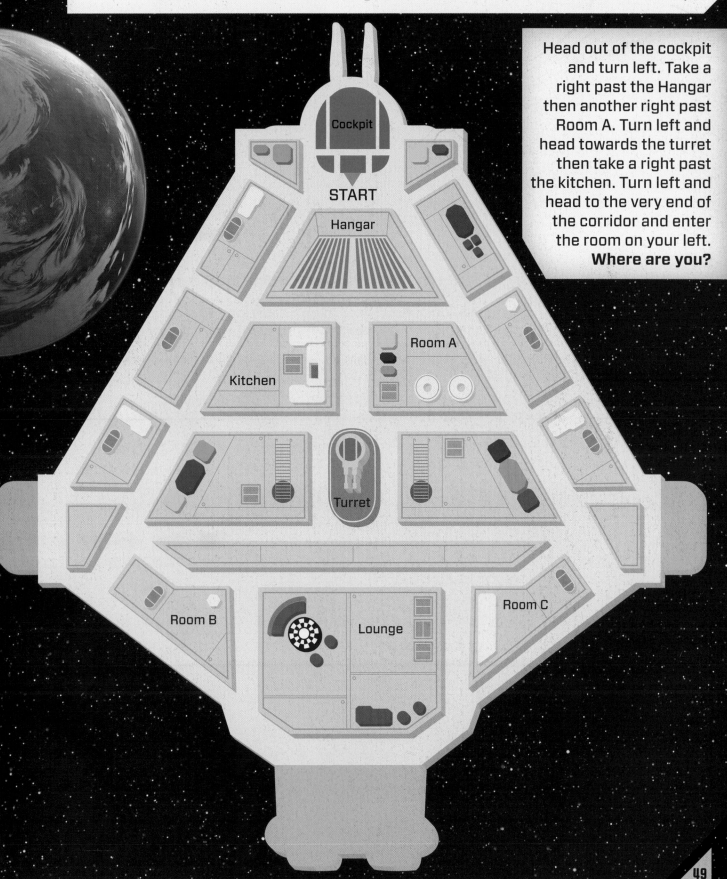

THE ESCAPE

CONTINUED FROM PAGE 41

1.

Aboard the *Ghost* the rebels argue over what to do about Ezra.
"It's our fault he was there … " Hera says.
"We just met this kid!" Zeb cries. "We're not going back for him!"
"They'll be waiting for us," Sabine chimes in. "We can't save him."

2.

Chopper beeps his agreement with Hera. "What did he say?" Zeb asks.
"He voted with me. That's two against two," Hera says. "Kanan, you have the deciding vote."
Kanan has a tough decision to make.

3.

Ezra tricks the troopers guarding his cell. He starts to make horrible choking sounds. The troopers barrel into the room to find it … empty. Ezra has sneaked behind them out of the cell and locked them in.

4.

Ezra enters a storeroom filled with various Imperial helmets and weapons. He tries on a cadet helmet and activates the built-in radio. He hears an Imperial officer report that the Wookiees will be off-loaded to work spice mine K-77.

5.

Suddenly an officer declares a security breach in the Lower Hangar.

"I don't know how," the officer continues, "but the rebel ship approached without alerting our sensors."

"They came back!" Ezra smiles to himself as he crawls through a airduct. "I don't believe it ... "

"Order all stormtroopers to converge on the Lower Hangar," Kallus commands. "I'll meet them there." Ezra has to help his new friends, so he poses as an Imperial on the radio to cause a diversion. "This is Trooper LS-123, reporting intruders in the Upper Hangar. I believe the Lower Hangar is a diversion."

"Maybe, maybe not," Kallus says. "Squads Five through Eight divert to Upper Hangar. The rest converge as ordered."

The rebels head into the bay ready to rescue Ezra, but he jumps down in front of them wearing the Imperial helmet before they can go any further. Zeb punches him.

"First you ditch me, then you hit me?!" Ezra cries.

"How was I supposed to know it was you?" Zeb says. "You were wearing a bucket!"

9.

Kallus and his troopers enter the hangar. Ezra throws his cadet helmet at them.

The rebel group run towards the *Ghost*. Kanan and Sabine shoot at the Imperials while Hera fires with the *Ghost*'s guns.

Ezra arms his slingshot, but before he can fire Zeb pushes him inside the ship. **"OH, NO. THIS TIME YOU BOARD FIRST!"**

10.

The *Ghost*'s ramp goes up and the ship takes off.

"Do not let them ... "Kallus shouts to the troopers as something catches his eye. There is a painted orange phoenix on the floor. He runs his hand over the image and sniffs it before realising what it is. His eyes widen in fear. **"TAKE COVER!"** he screams.

11.

Sabine smiles as she presses a button. The phoenix explodes and rips a hole in the floor of the Star Destroyer.

12.

Crates and troopers are being sucked into space. "Turn on the shield!" screams Kallus as he struggles to hold on. A trooper activates the emergency shield and seals the breach. A furious Kallus pulls himself up.

13.

The *Ghost* escapes into hyperspace. "**WELCOME ABOARD. AGAIN,**" Hera says to Ezra, relieved. "Thank you. I really didn't think you'd come back for me," Ezra says. "I know where they're really taking the Wookiees," he says as the rest of the rebels join them. "Have you heard of the Spice Mines of Kessel?"

14.

"Slaves sent there last a few months, maybe a year," Sabine says. "And for Wookiees born in the forest ... it's a death sentence," Zeb adds. "Then I guess we better go save 'em," Ezra says.

15.

Back on the Star Destroyer a trooper approaches Kallus holding Ezra's cadet helmet. "One of the rebels was using this helmet ... the transmitter was on." Kallus realises what the rebels' next move will be.

CONTINUES ON PAGE 60

ESCAPE FROM THE EMPIRE

The rebels are trying to escape the Imperial Transport Ship. Help them out by playing this game. The first player to escape the ship is the winner!

START

Kallus arrives.
Move back 2 spaces.

The *Phantom* comes to your
rescue. Move forward 3 spaces.

YOU WILL NEED:

• Something to act as counters (coins or buttons) • A die • 2-6 players

Zeb disarms a stormtrooper.
Have another go.

It's a trap!
Miss a turn.

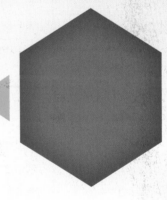

Sabine sets off an explosive.
Move forward 2 spaces.

FINISH

Ezra gets left behind.
Go back to the beginning.

MANDALORIAN MASTERPIECE

Sabine is a master of explosives, but also an expert artist. Copy this Mandalorian rebel's helmet and give it a new paint job. Be as creative as possible to do this graffiti girl proud!

MYSTERIOUS MESSAGE

Obi-Wan Kenobi delivers a very important message. Cross out all the weapons and characters in this grid to reveal his warning.

Our	Light~~sab~~er	Kanan	Jedi	Sabine
Bo-rifle	Order	Blaster	Kallus	And
Hera	Explosive	The	Ezra	Republic
Have	Chopper	Slingshot	Fallen	Zeb

ANSWER:

_____

_____

STARSHIP SHAPES

There are many starships above Lothal. Colour in the squares indicated by the coordinates below to reveal an Imperial vessel.

| A1 - A9 | B5 | C5 | D4 - D6 | E3 - E7 | F3 - F7 | G4 - G6 | H5 | I5 | J1 - J9 |

Enjoying the story so far? How much do you remember?

1. Who does Hera send to warn the crew about the trap?

_____

2. What does Ezra find in Kanan's room?

A. 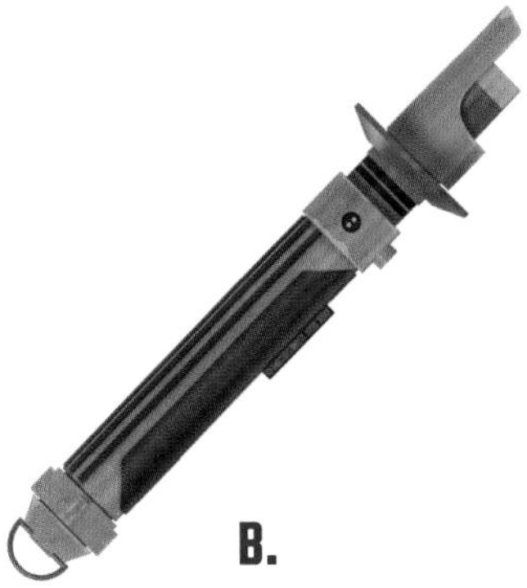   **B.**    **C.**

(circle the right object)

3. Kanan tells the crew about an Imperial ship full of banthas.

TRUE ◯   FALSE ◯

4. Who arrives to capture the rebels?

AGENT KALLUS   **THE INQUISITOR**   **COMMANDANT ARESKO**

(circle the right answer)

5. Who helps Sabine sabotage the Imperial transport?

_____

6. Zeb gets left behind.

TRUE ◯   FALSE ◯

THE RESCUE

CONTINUED FROM PAGE 53

1.

The *Ghost* arrives on Kessel to see Wookiees bound up and being herded along by stormtroopers. The ship swoops down and the rebels leap down the ramp. They take cover behind some crates to fight the troopers. Ezra scrambles towards the Wookiees and uses his astromech arm to free them from their binders. He starts to guide them back to the *Ghost* when three TIE fighters appear and begin firing.

2.

The *Ghost* must quickly escape when an Imperial transport ship arrives.
Kallus emerges from the transport with an enormous pack of stormtroopers.
"**TAKE THEM DOWN,**" Kallus commands.
A Wookiee child named Kitwarr runs off followed by a trooper. His father Wulffwarro calls out and tries to go after him, but is shot in the shoulder by a trooper. Zeb runs to help him.

3.

Kanan leaps over the crate and walks onto the battlefield. He removes his lightsaber from his belt and activates it. The troopers and Ezra are stunned. Kallus's fury building, he shouts, "All Troopers! Focus your fire on... the **JEDI!**"

Kanan expertly defends his friends from the gun fire using his lightsaber. "**TIME TO GO!**" he shouts. Zeb helps Wulffwarro on to the *Ghost*, but the Wookiee is crying out for his missing son. Ezra sees the Wookiee's distress and runs off in the direction of Kitwarr.

Kanan and Zeb look towards the catwalk in the distance. A small wookiee is being chased by a trooper, and coming up behind them... **EZRA!**

Kitwarr sees Ezra and cries out. The trooper turns and raises his blaster. Ezra, in an amazing, Jedi-like stunt, leaps through the air, somersaulting over the trooper and lands in front of Kitwarr. He fires his slingshot, disabling the trooper and knocking him off the railing. He turns to collect the young Wookiee, but suddenly, Kallus arrives.

"**IT'S OVER FOR YOU, JEDI!**" Kallus says. "A Master and an Apprentice, such a rare find these days!"
"I don't know where you get your delusions, bucket-head!" Ezra protests. "I work alone."
Just then, the *Ghost* rises up alongside the catwalk with Kanan standing on top, lightsaber at the ready. "**NOT THIS TIME,**" he says.

8.

Kallus fires at the Jedi, but Kanan deflects the shots back, knocking Kallus off the railing. **"JUMP, KID!"** Kanan calls, and Ezra and Kitwarr leap onto the ship. The *Ghost* flies away from Kessel and into the clouds.

9.

The *Ghost* docks with a Wookiee gunship, returning the proud prisoners to their people. Wulffwarro is happy and grateful to be reunited with Kitwarr. Sabine translates, "He says if we ever need help, the Wookiees will be there."

10.

As the last of the Wookiees depart, Ezra turns to the group. "So... I guess you drop me off next?" he asks. None of the rebels look happy about this. The *Ghost* heads back to Lothal.

11.

As the *Ghost* lands, Ezra bumps into Kanan, stealing his lightsaber again in the process. Ezra heads down the ramp, but Kanan stops him. "I think you have something that belongs to me," he says. Ezra reluctantly hands Kanan the holocron and runs away.

12.

Ezra arrives home at his tower. He senses Kanan is already behind him. "What's the Force?" he asks. "The Force is everywhere," Kanan explains. "And it's strong with you, Ezra. Otherwise, you'd never have been able to open the Holocron."

13.

"So, what do you want?" Ezra is defensive. "To offer you a choice. You can keep the lightsaber you stole – let it become just another dusty souvenir. Or you can give it back and come with us, come with me, and be trained in the ways of the Force. You can learn what it means to be a Jedi."

14.

Kanan leaves as quietly as he arrived. Back on the *Ghost* in his cabin he watches Obi-Wan's message. "We must persevere, and in time a new hope will emerge. May the Force be with you... **ALWAYS,**" Obi-Wan says. Suddenly the door opens and there stands Ezra.

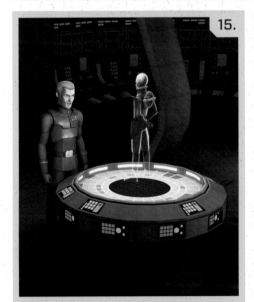

15.

On a Star Destroyer above Kessel, Kallus stands on the bridge addressing a hologram. "Excuse the intrusion, **INQUISITOR,**" he says. "But in the course of my duties, I have encountered a rebel cell. The leader of that cell made good use of a lightsaber."

16.

He looks up at the menacing figure of the master interrogator.
"Ah, Agent Kallus," the Inquisitor smiles. "**YOU DID WELL TO CALL.**"

THE END

FIRE FIGHT

Kallus and his troopers have the rebels surrounded, but Kanan has a surprise.
What does Kallus say to his army?

S E C I O T D J R H

F R P F U Y N A L

WOOKIEE WORDSEARCH

Find the following words about Wookiees in this wordsearch

H	W	N	X	Y	P	C	R	E	R	O
W	O	J	H	D	S	O	Y	R	N	R
T	F	R	A	D	G	W	A	O	Z	R
J	L	T	I	H	C	W	C	X	I	A
D	U	O	R	P	T	B	Z	S	D	W
Q	D	B	Y	T	Z	C	V	D	K	F
J	S	C	I	B	X	B	F	E	I	F
V	N	K	Q	K	E	S	S	E	L	L
K	A	S	H	Y	Y	Y	K	U	D	L
J	R	Y	W	O	O	K	I	E	E	U
C	R	E	N	O	S	I	R	P	V	W

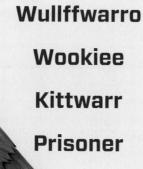

Wullffwarro   **Kessel**

Wookiee   **Kashyyyk**

Kittwarr   **Hairy**

Prisoner   **Proud**

DARING DEPARTURE

The rebels have a tough time getting the Wookiees away from Kessel with all those Imperials on their tail! Help them through by following the pattern around the maze, moving left, right, up or down, but not diagonally.

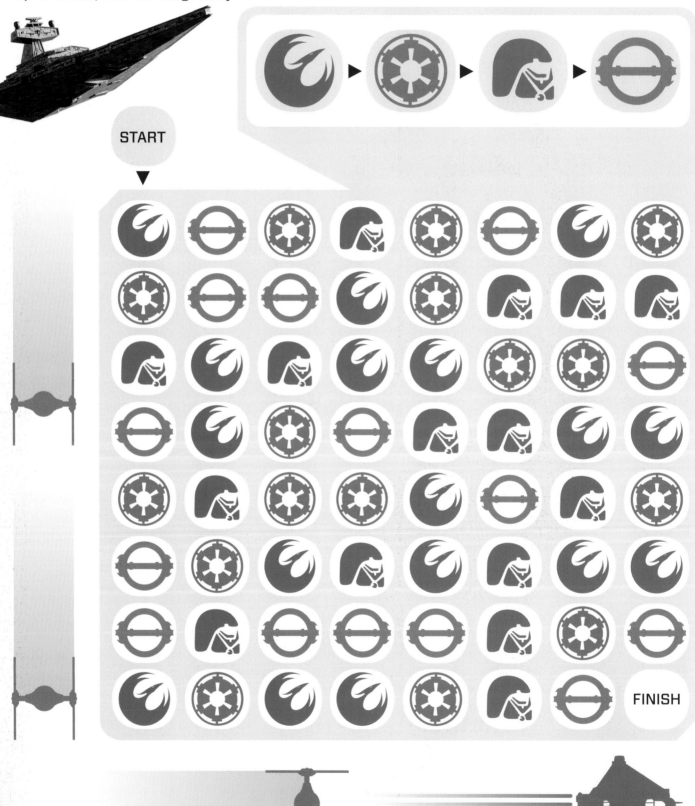

START

FINISH

RUTHLESS REFLECTION

Kallus calls the Inquisitor to help him capture the rebels. Finish the drawing of this menacing Imperial by drawing his other half and colouring it in.

ANSWERS

PAGE 18 MARKETPLACE MINDBENDERS:
1. THICK AND THINK
3. STREET VENDOR

PAGE 20 CRATE CONUNDRUM:

PAGE 21 WHO IS THAT KID?:

PAGE 22 HOT PURSUIT:

PAGE 25 CARGO CAPER:

PAGE 30 REBEL ORDER:

1. 2. 3. 4.

PAGE 31 SPACE SQUABBLE:
A LITTLE LESS ATTITUDE,
A LITTLE MORE ALTITUDE

PAGE 32 STORY TRIVIA PART ONE:
1. LOTHAL
2. GREEN
3. KANAN
4. VIZAGO
5. TRUE
6. WOOKIEES

PAGE 33 REBEL REVIEW:
KANAN: RECKLESS
HERA: CREATIVE
SABINE: GUTSY
ZEB: ANNOYING

PAGE 34 RUNAWAY REBEL:
PATH C

PAGE 37 TWIN TROUBLEMAKERS:

3.

PAGE 42 *GHOST* GRID:

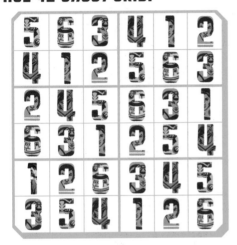

5	6	3	4	1	2
4	1	2	5	6	3
2	4	5	6	3	1
6	3	1	2	5	4
1	2	6	3	4	5
3	5	4	1	2	6

PAGE 43 LIGHTSABER SUMS:

C

PAGE 46 USE THE FORCE:

PAGE 49 FOLLOW THE FORCE:

ROOM B

PAGE 57 MYSTERIOUS MESSAGE:

OUR JEDI ORDER AND THE REPUBLIC HAVE FALLEN

PAGE 58 STARSHIP SHAPES:

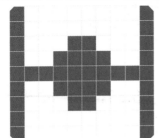

PAGE 59 STORY TRIVIA PART TWO:

1. EZRA
2. B (LIGHTSABER)
3. FALSE
4. AGENT KALLUS
5. CHOPPER
6. FALSE

PAGE 64 FIRE FIGHT:

ALL TROOPERS FOCUS YOUR FIRE ON THE JEDI.

PAGE 65 WOOKIEE WORDSEARCH:

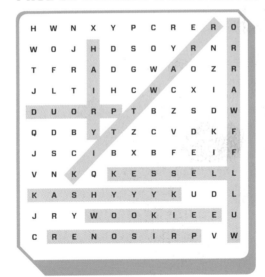

H	W	N	X	Y	P	C	R	E	R	O
W	O	J	H	D	S	O	Y	R	N	R
T	F	R	A	D	G	W	A	O	Z	R
J	L	T	I	H	C	W	C	X	I	A
D	U	O	R	P	T	B	Z	S	D	W
Q	D	B	Y	T	Z	C	V	D	K	F
J	S	C	I	B	X	B	F	E	I	F
V	N	K	Q	K	E	S	S	E	L	L
K	A	S	H	Y	Y	Y	K	U	D	L
J	R	Y	W	O	O	K	I	E	E	U
C	R	E	N	O	S	I	R	P	V	W

PAGE 66 DARING DEPARTURE: